W9-BEQ-853

THUNDER ON THE SIERRA

by Kathy Balmes

Illustrated by Vicki Catapano

SILVER MOON PRESS
NEW YORK

First Silver Moon Press Edition 2001
Copyright © 2001 by Kathy Balmes
Illustrations copyright © 2001 by Vicki Catapano
Edited by Carmen McCain

The publisher would like to thank Jim Rawls
of Diablo Valley College for historical fact checking.

All rights reserved.
No part of this publication may be reproduced,
except in the case of quotation for articles and reviews,
or stored in any retrieval system, or transmitted in any form
or by any means, electronic, mechanical, photocopying, recording,
or otherwise, without written permission from the publisher.

For information:
Silver Moon Press
New York, NY
(800) 874–3320

Library of Congress Cataloging-in-Publication Data

Balmes, Kathy.
    Thunder on the Sierra / by Kathy Balmes ; illustrated by Vicki Catapano.--1st Silver
Moon Press ed.
        p. cm. -- (Adventures in America)
    Includes bibliographical references.
    Summary: In 1852, recently orphaned, thirteen-year-old Mateo becomes an "arriero," or
mule driver, bringing supplies to California gold miners and searching for the notorious
bandit who stole his horse, but when he learns that Yankee squatters are threatening to
take the ranch he grew up on, Mateo heads for home.
    ISBN 1-893110-10-9
    1. Frontier and pioneer life--California--Juvenile fiction. [1. Frontier and pioneer
life--California--Fiction. 2. Mexican Americans--Fiction. 3. Mules--Fiction. 4. Gold
mines and mining--California--Fiction. 5. Robbers and outlaws--Fiction. 6.
Orphans--Fiction. 7. California--Fiction.] I. Catapano, Vicki, ill. II. Title. III. Series.

PZ7.B2136 Ye 2001
[Fic]--dc21   00-047023

10 9 8 7 6 5 4 3 2 1
Printed in the USA

For John

Thanks for supporting the arts,

Love, K

Introduction

California's first rancho owners, *rancheros*, were Spanish. A few came to California with explorers or the *padres* who founded the Spanish missions. Others came as soldiers to build the Spanish forts. The King of Spain granted them land in the 1700s. Although they spoke Spanish and their customs were Spanish, they thought of themselves as Californios, not Spaniards.

In 1822 a ship from Mexico brought the news that California no longer belonged to Spain but to the newly independent Mexico. The Mexican government gave many more land grants to retired soldiers, government officials, and other Mexican citizens.

In 1846 the United States declared war on Mexico. When the war ended in 1848, California belonged to the U.S. The Californios became American citizens and helped shape the state constitution. Around the same time, gold was discovered, and the next year ninety thousand impatient "forty-niners" rushed into California. The placer gold found at the surface of the land, however, was soon picked over. Thousands of hopeful miners were disappointed by the time this story begins in 1852.

ONE

ON MY OWN

IT WAS A WARM EVENING IN THE SUMMER of 1852. I stood in the shadows leaning against the strong shoulder of my father's palomino mare. Low voices and guitar music drifted into the stables from the rancho's patio, where dusty vaqueros smoked and talked after dinner. I wiped the tears on my cheek against the mare's golden coat and breathed in her comforting hay scent.

The jingle of boots dragging spurs announced two vaqueros entering the stable. I was thirteen and didn't want them to see me crying, so I quickly slid into the first hiding place I could find—under the manger.

The footsteps stopped outside the mare's stall. The palomino put her head over the lower half of the door and nickered.

"Fandango's a fine mare," said one of the vaqueros.

"Best horse on the rancho," agreed the second. "She may be the best horse in California for rounding up and roping cattle. She's quick as a cat. Big and beautiful, too, with that long white mane and tail and dark golden hide. Any man would be proud to have her."

"Fandango's too good for Mateo, no matter how great a vaquero old Miguel thinks the kid is," the first voice grumbled. "Mateo can't ride on his father being mayordomo any more. He's just like the rest of us now that his father is dead. The only thing that makes the boy different from us now is that horse."

My legs and back cramped, but I didn't move.

The first voice spoke again, "Fandango might wander off some night. I might just wander off with her."

"I wouldn't do that if I were you," his companion warned. "A few weeks ago I came across a man hung by the neck from a tree. He was still twitching. A sign on him read: 'Horse Thief.' Probably made a good meal for the vultures."

"I'm too smart to become buzzard bait," said the first voice.

"We'll see. Drool over the horse as much as you want, but I'm going to bed," said his companion as he left.

The thief remained, patting Fandango's satin neck. "How would you like to take me to Mexico, *mi querida?*" he whispered. "I could sell you for a fortune there." He walked off humming.

Blood pounded in my ears. Fandango was mine! She was the only family I had left. What was I going to do? That vaquero, whoever he was, could steal her while I was working on the range or sleeping. I hadn't recognized his voice, so I couldn't accuse anyone. Even Don Rafael, the rancho's owner, couldn't stop a thief from stealing a horse when no one was watching.

No one was going to take Fandango from me! I would leave with her now. I didn't have a plan, but I had plenty of anger to fuel my energy. Creeping out of the stable, I slipped along the rancho's long veranda in the twilight, past the kitchen, dining room, and chapel to the room my father and I had shared.

I was already wearing most of my clothes: leather chaps over my pants and a leather jacket over my shirt. After stuffing extra clothes and my father's pistols into my saddlebags, I hid his bowie knife in my high, horsehide boot and fingered my dead mother's rosary beads before dropping them into my pocket. The battered black sombrero, which kept the sun and rain off my face, I threw on top of the saddlebags.

I lay down to wait until everyone was asleep. When I closed my eyes, I again saw the scene of my father's death. He was roping a mare from a wild herd. He didn't ride Fandango because he didn't want the wild stallion leading the herd to try to steal her. I galloped after him. Suddenly his black gelding tripped. The gelding was moving so fast and was so big that he crashed headfirst into the ground. His hindquarters flew up, and he tumbled over onto his back, crushing my father under him.

I shook my head, trying to clear the memory and the familiar dull, empty ache in my heart.

When I thought it was safe, I crept to the storeroom and stuffed beans, dried beef, deer meat, chocolate, and tortillas into my saddlebags. I filled my cow's horn canteen with water, slung the saddlebags over my shoulder, and tiptoed to the stable.

In the dark I smoothed two saddle blankets over Fandango's back. I would use them as a bed on the trail. My hands shook as I swung the saddle up on the large mare, fastened the cinch, and tied on the saddlebags. I hurriedly bridled her and mounted. Fandango walked quietly past the corral that held the young horses in training. Thankfully, none of them neighed to her.

When we were too far from the rancho house to be heard, I let Fandango gallop. The big mare felt rested and strong under me. Her ears moved back and forth, questioning the night sounds. Moonlight shone on her silver mane, which swayed to the rhythm of her hoof beats.

We loped across open grassland past vast herds of deer, elk, and antelope. The wild animals looked at us, as if wondering whether we were fleeing a predator. Grizzly bears, mountain lions, and wolves still roamed California in the summer of 1852.

We didn't have a trail to follow, but it didn't matter. I just wanted to get away from the vaquero who was planning to steal Fandango. Maybe I was also trying to escape my grief over the loss of my father.

When Fandango was winded, I rested her in a small stand of twisted red manzanita, sharp leafed oak, and fragrant bay trees. The mare's hooves crunched the fallen leaves. Her head rose, and her nostrils widened, smelling for danger as she threaded

her way through the trees. Small night creatures scurried about. Something large swooped from a tree overhead. Fandango froze. She had reason to be afraid. Mountain lions drop from trees onto their prey.

"It's just a great horned owl," I said out loud, not sure whether I was talking to calm Fandango's fears or my own. I stroked her neck, where I could feel her pulse beating. From far away I heard a sound that made my blood freeze: wolves howling. I knew a pack of wolves would attack a man. I turned Fandango in the opposite direction, and she rushed out of the trees. We walked and jogged all night. I didn't know where we were going and didn't really care.

It was coldest before sunrise. The sweat in my shirt chilled my skin. As the sky lightened, the chirping of birds made a cheerful racket. Quail scurried along the ground with their chicks, scolding Fandango for disturbing them. Thousands of doves and wild pigeons cooed. Sunlight sparkled off the wings of a massive flock of birds that rose, dipped, and whirled before us on the wide plain.

After the showy sunrise, the sun warmed the dry herbs and grasses, and their aroma floated to me in waves. Above us hovered winged hunters. Small rodents, reptiles, and birds hid in thickets.

Fandango swung along at a walk, swishing her luxurious tail to brush off horseflies. Sometimes she twitched her skin or shook her neck to flick her mane. When smaller flies tried to drink from the moisture of her eyes, she tossed her thick forelock.

The day grew hot. I hadn't been careful to stay

near a river or stream, and now I wondered where I would find water.

I turned Fandango in two small circles to scare off any rattlesnakes that might be underfoot in the long grass and dismounted. The mare rubbed her head against me, asking me to take off the bridle. I remembered my father's words: "Trust your horse, Mateo."

Fandango's instinct would lead her to water. I pulled the bridle off and hung it on my saddle horn. I rubbed behind her itchy ears and brushed the flies away from her eyes. Taking a last gulp of water, I poured the rest into my cupped palm for the mare. She sniffed, lipped, and then licked the water from my hand.

I mounted, and Fandango, now without a bridle, started off in a new direction. The golden grass in the distance seemed to shimmer in the heat. I was hot, thirsty, and drowsy. Fandango probably felt the same.

Suddenly Fandango raised her head and pricked her ears toward a line of trees on the flat, dry grasslands. She took off at an eager lope. We rushed through the trees to what I figured was the San Joaquin River.

Fandango splashed into the shallows, wetting me with spray, and plunged her nose into the clear water. Slipping from the saddle, I bent to drink. Fandango's knees started to buckle. I slapped her belly with my open palm, startling her enough to make her stand up. "Oh no, you don't," I said. "My father's saddle may be banged up, but don't lie on it in the river. Wait a minute. I'll take it off so you can roll."

Undoing the cinch, I pulled the saddle and blankets off her hot, sweaty back and set them on a fallen tree on the riverbank. Fandango lay down in the water, grunting with joy as she splashed and rolled and rubbed her back on the sandy river bottom. It looked like so much fun that I tossed my sombrero onto the bank and dunked my head in the cool water, too.

When she finished rolling, Fandango stood up and shook like a dog, sending a shower of water in all directions. For the first time since my father's death, I smiled. I ran my fingers through my wet, heavy black hair and put my sombrero back on.

But we couldn't rest yet. What if that vaquero tracked us and stole Fandango? I reached down and touched the knife in my boot.

After saddling and bridling the wet horse, I rode her upstream in the river a long way. The mare enjoyed sloshing along the sandy bottom. If the thief were tracking us, he would see hoof prints where we entered the river. But we didn't come out of the river until I found a rocky place where her hooves would leave no prints.

Searching in the saddlebag as I rode, I pulled out a hard, black strip of beef jerky and thought about what to do next as I chewed.

"Think it out, Mateo. Make a plan," my father had often said.

Where could I hide?

I gazed across the dry, brown grasslands toward

the Sierra Nevada foothills. The gold country! I would hide in the crowds of gold seekers. I could find a job helping a blacksmith. My father had taught me how to shoe horses and mules. Or I could hunt for rabbits and other small game to sell to hungry prospectors. Maybe I'd try my luck panning for gold.

I had wanted to join the gold rush ever since 1848 when I read the story of the gold discovery in the *Californian,* a San Francisco newspaper. Many of the vaqueros left the rancho to look for gold the day after that article came out.

"Let's go too," I urged my father.

He shook his head. "They're fools. These cattle are the true riches. You'll see, Mateo."

He had been right. Before 1848 there had been so many cattle and so few people in California that beef was almost worthless. Rancheros sold the hide and tallow of a steer for three or four dollars each. But during the gold rush of 1849, the flood of hungry new miners wanted beef so badly that they paid fifty dollars or much more for a steer.

Some of the young vaqueros who had gone off to the gold camps later returned to the rancho, disgusted with the lawlessness and prejudice of the Yankee gold seekers. They advised friends and relatives to stay on the rancho.

I rode along the San Joaquin River that evening. Finally, so tired that I was afraid I might fall out of the saddle, I halted Fandango and dismounted. I untied the braided leather hobbles from my father's saddle. After pulling the bridle and saddle off, I led the mare by a hunk of mane until I found a grassy spot. I fastened the two loops of the hobbles around her front legs. With her legs loosely tied together, she could only take short steps. She could graze, but she would stay nearby. My father had trained her to come when he whistled. But I wasn't good at whistling, and I wasn't sure she would come to me.

After piling a mound of dry grass under a bay tree and spreading a saddle blanket over it, I collapsed. It felt wonderful to lie down and let my tense muscles relax.

For two more days I kept the trees along the river in sight as we walked and loped through flat grasslands. I saw no sign of anyone following me. On the third day I saw Stockton across the river.

Stockton, a booming trading town of over five thousand people, was mainly made of canvas tents. The bang of hammers and the grating of saws mixed with the shouts of mule drivers and miners. Stockton was the final stop for supply boats traveling up the San Joaquin River from San Francisco Bay. Burly laborers transferred cargoes onto large freight wagons drawn by mule teams. Freight wagons, horse-drawn carts, stagecoaches, and mule trains carried the supplies south to Mariposa and east to Sonora— to the gold country. Manure from the many horses and mules used to transport supplies gave the streets of Stockton a distinct aroma.

I rode around looking for work. I tried livery stables and general stores. No luck. Some men stared with envy at my flashy palomino as I rode by.

"That your horse?" called a red-haired boy.

"Yes," I answered in English. "Where can I find a blacksmith's shop?"

"Go to the end of the street and turn left," he answered. "Nice horse."

"Thanks."

I let Fandango drink from the water trough outside the blacksmith's shop before tying her to the hitching post and entering the shop. The blacksmith was bent over a horse's hoof.

When he straightened I said, "Do you need a helper? I know how to shoe horses."

The brawny man looked me over. I wasn't very big.

"No. Try the mining camps. I've heard they need a shoer in Sonora."

"Thanks."

When I came out of the blacksmith's shop, an elegantly dressed young man, who looked about twenty, was stroking Fandango's neck. The handsome Mexicano wore pants with jingling silver ornaments, a red sash around his waist, silver-mounted pistols on his hips, a short black jacket with silver buttons, and a black sombrero. His saddle was trimmed with silver. His bay horse looked well bred but not as beautiful as my palomino.

His glittering black eyes studied Fandango. "That's a magnificent horse. She yours?"

"Mine," I replied with pride.

"Where did you get her?" asked the young man.

I was eager to talk about my mare. "My father

bought her on our journey from Mexico. Her mother came from palominos that were bred at the Mission San Antonio de Padua."

"Yes. That mission was famous for their golden coated horses," said the man, nodding.

"My father spent all our money to buy her. She was only a year old. Already she was large and beautiful," I said.

"Did your father train her?"

"Yes. My father was an expert horseman. She responds to the slightest touch of the reins, pressure of the knees, or sway of the rider. When my father rode, horse and rider seemed the same creature. He said riding her was like dancing. That's why he called her Fandango, after the dance. My father is dead. She's mine now."

I stopped, afraid I had said too much to a stranger.

"Sorry about your father," said the man. He untied his horse and mounted in a smooth motion. "*Adiós*."

I rode out of Stockton, east toward the gold camps. I was tired and discouraged. I had no idea things were about to get much worse.

TWO

The Bandit Murieta

STAGECOACHES, OX CARTS, HORSES, AND mules had worn a road through the parched summer grasslands. The wide dirt path was flat and straight except where it dipped into creek beds and snaked around small stands of oak trees.

An hour out of Stockton, Fandango suddenly spun around to face riders galloping up behind us. She froze with her head high and neighed to the approaching horses. The setting sun set fire to her golden hide. A light breeze rippled her silver-white mane.

"A magnificent horse," the leader said when he reached me. I recognized the handsome young man who had admired Fandango in Stockton. The men with him were dirty and looked dangerous. They circled me menacingly. Several of them drew pistols and pointed them directly at me.

"Now, Joaquín?" a man on a stocky pinto asked the young bandit leader. The man held his gun strangely; he was missing a finger.

"No," said Joaquín sharply.

He spoke to me calmly. "Get off the horse and give me the reins."

My heart hammered against my ribs. I had no choice: Get off or be shot off. I dismounted and with trembling hands gave up the reins. I backed away.

"Juan, search his saddle bags. Take any guns you find," said Joaquín.

A rough looking man, with a large mole on his sweaty cheek, dismounted, walked toward me, reached down, and drew my bowie knife from my boot. He pushed his other grubby hand into my saddlebags and threw my clothes to the ground. He grunted with pleasure when he felt my father's pistols.

"Give me those," the three-fingered bandit ordered. His eyes narrowed to slits.

"No! Joaquín said I could have them," whined Juan.

In a flash the three-fingered bandit fired four bullets into Juan's chest. "Wrong," he said coolly.

Juan fell backward, twitched, and lay limp. Blood from the dead man's wounds seeped into the dirt.

The three-fingered bandit aimed his smoking gun at me. He spoke with brutal detachment. "Now it's your turn, boy. Run. I need target practice."

I didn't run. But I tensed, expecting a bullet.

"No!" shouted Joaquín. He aimed his silver pistol at the three-fingered bandit. His dark eyes blazed. "I am leader here. Have you forgotten?"

The three-fingered bandit grudgingly lowered his gun.

Joaquín lowered his gun more slowly.

The bandit leader turned and studied me as the

three-fingered bandit dismounted to collect my pistols and knife from the body. "You remind me of myself at your age. You're not as handsome as I was, but you had a better horse than I ever did," he said with a flash of white teeth.

"Yesterday, we discovered a man who was tracking you. We heard him shoot a rabbit and surprised him while he was cooking it. He tried to make a deal for his life: He told me he could take me to the best horse in California. He showed me your tracks. I said 'no deal,' shot him, and took his horse." Joaquín turned back to the three-fingered bandit, who had re-mounted, and the rest of the band. "¡Vámanos!"

They left me in a cloud of dust with the discarded clothes and the body. I knew I should bury the dead man. But I didn't. My chest was tight with anger. I had a strong urge to kick the dead man with the pointed toe of my boot, over and over. It would have been satisfying. Instead I rolled up my clothes and started walking toward Sonora. I wasn't taking any more chances. I stayed off the road in case Joaquín or the three-fingered bandit decided to come back and shoot me.

I hated walking. I wasn't used to it. *Should I head back to the rancho?* I wondered. I thought I probably should.

I liked being a vaquero. Most days I left the rancho after breakfast and didn't return until sundown. There were no fences. I spent my days riding along the boundary line of the neighboring ranchos, looking for stray cattle and horses. All finding, herding, holding, and branding of cattle was done on horseback. Three rancho horses were mine to use.

I liked the rambling, one-story house that formed a square around a large patio. In the evenings I sat on a smooth wooden bench against the cool, white adobe wall under the veranda, listening to the other vaqueros talk of their day's work with cattle and horses. Life was busy but not hurried. Neighbors came to the many fiestas and fandangos, some of which lasted for days.

I liked the people at the rancho. Californios were well known for their kindness and hospitality to friends and strangers. They loved fine manners, clothes, and horses. I woke most mornings to the sound of Doña Dolores singing a sunrise song. After breakfast, her husband, the ranchero Don Rafael, stood on the porch and talked with the new mayordomo, Miguel, about what had to be done that day. Old Miguel had been a good friend to my father, and he was kind to me.

I could go back to the rancho now that I knew the bandit had killed the vaquero who was tracking me. But Fandango! She was the whole reason I had left the rancho. I would not return until I had my father's horse. I didn't know how I would get her back, but I would or I'd die trying.

What would my father advise? He would stroke his thick, black mustache as he often did when he had something important to say. His eyes would crinkle at the corners in smile lines, and he would tell me, "Patience, Mateo. There is a proper time for everything."

Now was not the time to rescue Fandango. I had to find food and water. The bandits hadn't left me any.

I followed what I hoped was a trail but was probably only a deer path. Grass grew over it in places. I knew Sonora was in the foothills, so I wasn't close. But I could tell from the setting sun at my back that I was traveling east, toward the southern part of the gold country.

A full moon rose, and the night turned cold. I could see well enough to walk. I was used to going without food for long stretches, but I would need water soon. Fear and doubt nagged at me. Did this part of the country have bears or wolves? Was I even heading the right way?

I trudged on through the unchanging night landscape. When I was too tired to walk any further, I collapsed on the grass and slept.

My situation looked no brighter in the morning, although I could see the foothills in the distance. I plodded on through grass and shrubs. The familiar smell of warm tarweed and the buzz of insects surrounded me. The summer sun made the land desert-like. My throat and tongue were dry. I was weak with hunger.

In the late afternoon the grassy ground sloped up to rolling hills. Hiking up the tallest hill around, I peered at the horizon surrounding me. Far to the east, the grasslands gave way to rolling oak woodland. As I turned back to the west, I saw something that gave me hope.

A mule train was snaking its way among the low hills from the direction of Stockton. I counted twelve mules tied loosely together. They were all in good condition, sleek and fat. Each mule had a bit of red, blue, or yellow on its bulging packsaddle. The cheerful colors stood out against the miles of golden hills. At the front was a muleskinner, an arriero. He wore the sombrero, white shirt, and white pants that were the uniform of many northern Mexicanos. His cheerful voice, as he urged his mules on, mixed with the tinkling of a bell around the lead mule's neck. It wasn't until they were close that I could make out the arriero's words.

"Cisco, you dunghill, move along. Jobo, you're a filthy beast with fleas for friends. Keep up. Gina, you feather brained carcass, walk straight. Hey, Elsa, excess of stupidity, get back in line." The old arriero insulted the mules in a calm, soothing voice.

"Whoa, mules," said the arriero when he reached me. The old man watched as the mules came to a halt. One near the end of the line stopped suddenly. The mule behind him laid back her long ears and bared her yellow teeth.

"Sabana, spawn of a rattlesnake, don't bite that butt in front of you. Pia, you putrid pile of dung, stand still."

When all the mules had stopped, the old arriero looked at me. "Are you lost, boy?"

"No. Bandits stole my horse."

The elderly Mexicano looked me over. The lids

over his watery eyes, drooped. His skin was lined like an old boot. "Walk with us," he said kindly. "Were you riding to the Sonoran camp?"

"Yes."

"It is a long way up in the foothills. My name is Pedro. My mules call me No Go Pedro."

The small, wrinkled man seemed a little crazy, but I liked him.

No Go Pedro gave me water and several pieces of jerky. I soon felt stronger.

"Walk on, mules," called the arriero.

I hiked next to the large brown mule Pedro rode.

"What did those bandits look like?" he asked.

"I think they were all Mexicanos or Californios. The leader was young, maybe nineteen or twenty, well dressed, and handsome. Another bandit was missing a finger on his right hand."

"Ahhh! Three-Fingered Jack. Manuel García is his real name. An American shot off a finger on his right hand during the war with Mexico. He's vicious and bloodthirsty. The leader was most likely Joaquín Murieta."

"Yes. One of the bandits called him Joaquín," I said.

"Did you have a good horse?" the old man asked. "Murieta only steals the finest horses."

"Fandango is a beautiful palomino. Well trained by my father. I'll get her back," I said.

"I wouldn't count on it. You're lucky Murieta didn't shoot you. I've heard Murieta cuts out people's hearts. There are many stories about the great bandit Murieta.

Never met the man myself. I stay off the well traveled roads," said the arriero.

"Murieta might as well have cut out my heart. He took my horse, the only thing that matters to me. He left me without a gun, knife, food, or water," I said bitterly.

"You're alive. That's something," said the old man. He started talking to his mules again. "Fabio, you frothy mouthed fool, keep up or I won't give you any more chewing tobacco. It'll rot your teeth anyway. Rufo, you're as ugly as a bear's butt. Stay in line. Inez, you wad of snot, walk faster."

That evening I helped No Go Pedro unpack his mules. The old man's fingers were stiff. He was bowlegged and walked slowly. But he took great care to rub and brush each mule after he took off its load. He had a fresh insult for each one, which he lovingly whispered into its long ear. He made sure the mules were comfortably hobbled and happily grazing before he cooked his own meal. *Just like my father would have done,* I thought with a pang.

I made a campfire. We shared tortillas and a seasoned stew the old arriero made from beef jerky and pinto beans. The night grew cold. Belly full, I fell asleep by the dying fire, listening to the faint rhythm of the mules cropping grass.

I woke to the smell of chocolate. Pedro had cooked delicious frijoles. We ate the beans with tortillas and drank our chocolate. After breakfast, I helped Pedro pack the mules.

"You are familiar with packing a Spanish pack-saddle. Good. It allows the mule to carry more weight with not so many problems," commented Pedro as he watched me.

"My father taught me," I said.

"He taught you well. Is he an educated man?"

"My father was the mayordomo of a rancho. The ranchero, Don Rafael, hired a tutor to teach my father English so that he could trade with the ship captains who sailed around Cape Horn from Boston. My father traded cowhides and tallow for fine clothes, food, and other luxuries. He taught me English as he learned it."

"It is useful to know both English and Spanish. Where is your father?"

"He was killed in an accident."

"Sorry," said Pedro.

After Pedro started the mule train, I told him about my father's death and my last few days. I trudged beside his mount, Cisco. I had blisters on my feet, but I didn't complain. Each of the mules already carried two hundred pounds of food and supplies for the mining camps.

We unpacked and rested the team at noon. We ate while they grazed. It felt good to have someone to talk to. The old arriero chatted as much as I did. He spoke mostly about the mules.

"How did you name your mules?" I asked.

"I named them after people I know. That way I can insult those people as often as I like, and they'll never find out. My mules don't take the insults personally. They really are fine mules. They're all from Mexico. Mexicanos breed the best mules because they breed mares that are sound, compact, and spirited to donkeys. The offspring get the mare's body with the jack's legs, feet, and ears. And they're smart. A dumb mule, if there is such a thing, is smarter than a smart horse. They don't waste their energy pawing or running off here and there like horses," said Pedro.

I kept my opinion of mules to myself. I thought mules were ugly, lazy, stubborn, and stupid. I couldn't understand why anyone would breed a good mare to a donkey. My father had known my opinion and never let me work with mules. "You are not patient enough, Mateo. A mule needs kind treatment more than any other living creature and gets less."

After the mules were rested, we repacked them and started down the trail. Pedro, finally noticing my lack of interest in the topic of mules, told me stories about the mining camps he had visited. The stands of madrone, oak, and pine became larger as we left the grasslands behind and traveled toward the foothills of the Sierra Nevada.

That evening, No Go Pedro shot a jackrabbit in the large grassy meadow surrounded by oaks where we camped. We had another fine dinner. After a final check of the mules, we settled down for the night by the dying fire.

The braying of a mule jolted me awake. I opened my eyes to see a large shape leap upon the sleeping arriero. The old man shouted and covered his head and neck with his arms. A mountain lion! The big tawny killer was trying to get at his throat. The mules sent up a loud chorus of braying as they wheeled around in panic.

With a pounding heart, I jumped up and ran toward the mountain lion shouting and waving my arms, hoping to scare it away. It ignored me. I searched the dark ground frantically. Surely the arriero would have kept a gun near him as he slept. I saw it, grabbed it, and shot. The mountain lion sprang away from the arriero and ran into the night. Pedro swore in pain. I had shot him in the leg.

THREE

A Shattered Leg

PEDRO CONTINUED TO SWEAR IN BOTH Spanish and English, as I started a fire and examined his leg. The bullet had shattered his kneecap. I used a piece of my shirt to dig out the bullet, which was slippery with blood. The old arriero, his face contorted in agony, spouted new swear words as I pulled the bullet out.

My heart was in my throat. I had nearly killed the man by accident. "I'm sorry," I choked.

"No, no, Mateo. You don't know my gun. Sometimes it has a mind of its own. You had to shoot at the mountain lion, or it would have killed me. Look," said Pedro, showing me the deep gashes in his arms and chest. His wrists bled from the mountain lion's bites.

I hurried to an oak tree and felt the north side of its trunk for soft tufts of moss. I peeled the moss off the tree and brought it to Pedro. "An old Indian, who braided leather *reatas* at the rancho, told me that oak moss will help stop the bleeding," I explained.

The old man grunted approval.

I laid the green moss on his wounds.

"There are bandages in that pack by the fire," the arriero gasped.

I built up the fire and bandaged the old man. The mules calmed down and began to graze. I didn't like the sallow look of the arriero's skin or the sweat beaded on his forehead. His breathing was labored.

"How far are we from Sonora?" I asked.

"Two shakes of a mule's tail," Pedro said with a vain attempt at a smile. "We'll come to it the day after tomorrow. I can stay there at my brother's house. Get some sleep."

I lay down and closed my eyes. But my mind raced. What about the mules? What about the supplies for the camps? Would No Go Pedro ever recover enough to take his mules on the trail again? I heard my father's voice: "Think it through, Mateo. Make a plan."

By morning I had my plan. I would take over the mule train. And while I was helping the old man, I could talk to miners and maybe find out where Murieta's hiding place was.

I fixed a breakfast of tortillas, beans, deer jerky, and chocolate. After we ate, I packed the mules carefully, with direction from Pedro. I gently helped the arriero onto his mule. His wrinkled face looked pinched and pale under his sombrero.

I missed his cheerful insults as we started out. The mules did too. They didn't follow well. The last mule didn't follow at all. He stood still, looking sour. He had a black stripe across his shoulders and down his back. His nose, legs, mane, and tail were black. His body was the color of dried oat hay.

The old man glanced back at the mule. "Did you give Fabio his chewing tobacco?"

"No," I answered. "I've never heard of a mule that chews tobacco."

"This one does. Won't go without it. It's in his pack."

I found the chewing tobacco, put a wad on my palm, and thrust it under Fabio's nose. The mule took the tobacco with his lips and began chewing. Tobacco juice dribbled from his muzzle. *Stupid, ugly mule*, I thought.

"I forgot to tell you our deal," said the arriero when I returned to walk beside him. "Fabio keeps the end of the line moving as long as I supply him with a wad of chewing tobacco every morning. If I run out, I'm in for a long, slow day, and I might get kicked."

I walked beside the arriero's mule, Cisco, in silence for a long time. Finally the old man started talking. "Now I'll have to sell all my supplies at Sonora. I don't make a profit unless I reach the camps that only mules can pack into. The miners in those camps depend on my mule train for food and supplies."

"I could be your arriero. Yesterday, you said I'm good at packing mules. I could take over your mule train until you get well," I suggested.

"You are very young," said No Go Pedro. He didn't say anything for several minutes. His mule stumbled. The jolt made the old man wince in pain.

"All right. I think I can trust you. Anyway, I don't

have much choice. I can't travel through the winter on this leg. I'll teach you each mule's name and habits by the time we reach Sonora."

I chuckled inwardly at myself: me, an arriero. I didn't even like mules. Now I wouldn't be able to look for gold or Fandango. Still, I wouldn't starve. And I wouldn't have to walk.

The hills sloped up as we traveled east through scraggy pines. The next afternoon we saw the hilly town of Sonora in the distance. Sonora was not the busy mining town I had imagined. I saw canvas tents, rough-hewn wooden cabins, and fandango halls but not many people.

"I thought there would be more action in Sonora," I commented.

"There used to be," No Go Pedro said.

The old arriero explained that when news of gold first reached the state of Sonora, in northern Mexico, many thousands of Sonorans packed up their mules and came to California. They built a town in 1848 and named it after their home in Mexico. The Sonorans knew how to mine, and they did well. They willingly shared their wisdom and experience with the Americanos and Californios who arrived later. There was plenty of gold for everyone.

"Sonora was a wild, happy town a few years ago," he said with a far away look in his watery eyes. "The huts and shacks were bright with fabric streamers. Many Sonorans brought their women, too. The town smelled of spicy, home-cooked food. Music of guitars, banjos, and fiddles mixed with singing and braying.

A fandango was always going on. Anyone was welcome, Spanish-speaking or not."

"What happened?" I asked.

The old arriero shook his head sadly and explained how in 1849 thousands of gold seekers flooded the area. It became harder to find gold. Frustrated Yankee miners felt they should have what there was. Had America not just won the short war with Mexico over California? The Yankees resented that the Spanish-speaking miners, who had arrived first, had the best claims. They called all Sonorans, Chileans, Peruvians, and even the Californios who were U.S. citizens, "greasers."

"But the Yankees couldn't make them leave," I protested.

"Sometimes the Yankees attacked Spanish-speaking miners and ran them off their claims. If an injustice was done to a 'greaser,' it went unpunished. I've heard that Yankees threw Joaquín Murieta off his claim near Sonora. That started his life of crime."

The Yankee miners found other ways to force Californios out. In 1850 California became a state of the U.S. The new state legislature imposed the Foreign Miner's Tax. Spanish speakers had to pay twenty dollars a month if they wanted to look for gold. By 1850 many miners hardly *earned* twenty dollars a month.

"Some desperate Mexicanos like Murieta stole or killed to get money and food. Thousands returned to Mexico," the arriero said, shaking his head.

"But you didn't return to Mexico," I commented.

"No," he answered quietly. "I love California. It is some of the people I dislike."

As we neared the town, Pedro spoke again. "The merchants in Sonora lost customers when the Mexicanos left. The Foreign Miner's Tax was struck down. But Sonora is not the town it once was. I hope they still have a doctor here."

We walked to the end of the main street and stopped the mule train at the home of Pedro's brother. Emilio, a younger, straighter version of Pedro, sent his little boy for the doctor. His wife readied a bed while we eased Pedro from the mule and helped him into the house.

I camped outside of town with the mules. The next morning Emilio's son came to watch the mules while I returned to town to talk with Pedro.

Pedro looked small and withered in the clean white bed. He grinned when I entered his room.

"How are you, Pedro?"

"Better. The doctor has been here. He says to stay off my leg until spring."

Pedro gave me a tattered map to the camps where I should sell the supplies. I read the names of the gold camps out loud, "Hog Pen, Soap Root, Poor Man, Plug Ugly, Starvation, Total Wreck, Ever Ready, Old Stiff, Lost Dog, True Blue, Tip Top, Butcher Shop, Poverty Hill, Indian Gulch, Pay Day, and Dead Horse."

"Go to Dead Horse Camp first. I haven't been there for three months. There will be new camps that are not on my map," Pedro added.

I asked for ink and paper to write down his instructions.

He looked at me with pleased surprise. "You can read and write? Your father did teach you well."

Pedro told me how much to charge for each item in the mules' packs. He taught me the value of various coins.

"You will be paid mostly in gold dust. That's what the miners have. A pinch of dust is worth a dollar. A pinch is the amount a man can pick up between his forefinger and his thumb. Let me see your fingers," said Pedro.

I held up my short, stubby fingers, so like my father's.

"Perfect. You'll be able to pick up a large pinch with those. When you get low on supplies, go back to Stockton." Pedro told me where to buy supplies, what to buy, and how much to pay.

"Here is my bowie knife, my Kentucky rifle, and my pistol. The loaded mules will attract bandits and lawless miners. You'll need some practice shooting before you leave Sonora."

I nodded seriously. A smile played around Pedro's mouth. He was probably thinking of the last time I fired his pistol.

Pedro quickly moved on to the subject of his mules. "The most the mules can go, on the flat, is fifteen miles a day. But the ground you will be covering will not be flat. Your route is a loop, which will take you into the lower Sierra and back. Stop and unpack the mules after five hours. Let them graze. After your siesta, repack them and go on until nightfall. Never pack more than 225 pounds on any of them. Line them up in the order I showed you. It's best. They are good mules. Treat them kindly."

With those words, I became an arriero.

I spent the afternoon shooting Pedro's rifle and pistol at rotten apples. I knew it would be quite different to shoot a man. Could I do it?

At dawn I packed the mules and headed out of town. I rode Cisco, the brown mule Pedro always rode. He was bigger than the other mules. He was more like his mother, a horse, than his father, a donkey, so he was the best mule for riding. Gina came next. She was mouse-colored and the fattest mule in the team. A bell hung around her neck and jingled in time with her steps and the nodding of her head. The other mules were roped behind her and followed her bell.

My arm, back, and shoulder muscles soon ached from lifting on and taking off the heavy packs and packsaddles of eleven mules twice each day.

We traveled through steep hills, scattered with oak and pine trees and heavy brush on the way to Dead Horse Camp. Our path took us near gullies and gulches known as "dry diggings." Since it was late in the summer and no rain had fallen since early spring, it was dry and dusty. Sometimes we saw a lone miner working in a space only a few feet wide. His head would pop up, like a prairie dog out of its hole, at the sound of Gina's bell.

It took us two weeks to travel to Dead Horse Camp because the rocky hills were difficult for the mules to climb. I lost the narrow, overgrown trail several times. We reached the camp on a cloudy afternoon.

Tents and crudely made wood shacks clustered near a stream in a gully where the men panned for gold. The mules carefully stepped down a narrow trail to get to the camp. Stones that their hooves knocked off the trail clattered into the gully. Gina's bell announced our arrival. The happy shouts of miners echoed through the narrow valley. The young men in their teens and twenties all wore dirty flannel shirts and wool pants tucked into boots. They topped their outfits with wide-brimmed felt hats. Most men had bristly, bushy beards. I didn't see any women.

The whole camp hurried to meet us. They were all Yankees. They only spoke English.

I was nervous about charging the correct amounts for the goods. I wondered if the miners would try to cheat me since I was only thirteen. The prices I had to charge seemed outrageous to me: one dollar for an onion or one pound of potatoes, two dollars for a pound of dried apples. Coffee was four dollars a pound. But the miners cheerfully paid their coins or pinches of gold dust and asked me for news.

I didn't know what to say to the Yankee men. I was too shy to camp with them and a little afraid. There were over twenty Yankees in the camp. They might shoot me and take the mules and supplies. I remembered what Pedro had said about crimes done to "greasers" going unpunished.

When my sales were finished, I packed up the mules and traveled east through pine and cedar forests. When night came, I camped alone in a clearing—just the ornery, stubborn mules and me. I thought about my father and how I was no closer to finding his horse. That night the first storm of the fall hit.

FOUR

PLUG UGLY

TWO WEEKS LATER IT WAS STILL RAINING. The mules weren't cooperating. I was soaked and shivering. I had a cold. And it was my fourteenth birthday. I was feeling very sorry for myself.

I had hoped to make ten miles that day, but we were entering the Sierra Nevada mountain range. Its snowy peaks ran north and south the length of California. These high mountains had discouraged Yankees from coming to California before the gold rush.

I wanted to hurry to the next camp, so I traveled all day instead of giving the mules a break to graze in the afternoon. I had pushed the mules and skipped their siesta for the last three days. They started kicking at me when I loaded them, so I carried a whip. I knew they were tired and irritable. But so was I.

The mules were the opposite of my beautiful, willing, and obedient Fandango. Even the sight of them annoyed me. And they knew it.

It was Fabio who rebelled. Late in the afternoon, the thin, muddy trail zigzagged up a steep hill. Fabio stopped at every turn in the trail. I had to get off Cisco, slide down the wooded slope to the end of the line, and lead Fabio around the corner while shouting at the other mules to go forward a few steps.

I lost patience after the third time. I took the whip with me when I slid down to Fabio. I cracked the whip behind him to drive him on. Snap! He laid back his ears but stayed rooted to his spot. I tried again. Snap! Snap! He ignored me. All of my frustrations overwhelmed me at that moment: my father's death, the loss of Fandango, and being cold and sick and stuck in the middle of nowhere on my birthday with twelve stubborn mules. I whipped Fabio's butt, not once, but many times. I stepped closer and lashed his back legs. Fabio suddenly took two steps back and kicked me. It was a solid hit—the metal of his shoe to the bone of my knee. Then he strolled up to the mule in front of him and nipped her playfully on the rear. I collapsed in pain, uttering some of the swear words I had learned from Pedro.

I sat on the wooded slope in the pouring rain for quite a while. I heard my father's voice, "Patience, Mateo. Make a plan."

Finally I got to my feet, limped painfully up the hill, mounted Cisco, turned him, and rode back down the hill. The other mules followed. At the bottom I took off their packs and hobbled them where they could graze. I was careful not to walk where Fabio could kick me. I made camp under a canopy of ponderosa pine trees. My knee swelled and throbbed painfully.

We stayed until it stopped raining at noon of the next day. The clouds cleared, and the sun shone brightly. Steam rose from the wet mules. When I packed them, they smelled like old, damp blankets. I gave Fabio his wad of chewing tobacco. The rested team zigzagged willingly up the muddy hill.

From that day forward, I treated the mules kindly. As soon as they were no longer afraid of me, they stopped trying to kick me. I started talking to the mules as we traveled. They turned their ears to listen.

In fact, the only talking I did was to mules. After a month, I began to wonder if my solitary life as an arriero was making me crazy. I had been to many small camps, and sold most of my supplies, but I had not visited with the miners. I entered the camp of Plug Ugly ready to be sociable. Not just because I was lonely: I wanted to find Murieta.

Plug Ugly deserved its name. It had no trees. Sheer gray cliffs cast shadows over the camp most of the day. Large holes, dug by miners looking for gold, dotted the camp. The cliffs were pitted where miners had used Bowie knives to pry off pieces of rock as they searched for pockets of gold. A thin stream trickled through a rocky riverbed.

The miners were glad to see me. Two young men, a few years older than I, joined the line to purchase supplies. I tried to be friendly.

"Any luck?" I asked the younger of the two in English. His oat colored hair fell over light blue eyes and freckles. He was too young to grow a beard.

"Only a little. Most of the loose placer gold is

gone," he answered. "We've been coyoting—digging holes like coyotes do—to find gold. Have you ever wanted to look for gold?" he asked.

"Yes, often. But I am responsible for these mules. I have a route to follow and people waiting for food and supplies. Could I watch you?"

"Sure. It's hard work if you do it all day. Your back and arms ache. Your skin sunburns in the summer. You freeze in the winter. Mosquitoes and fleas eat you alive. Poison oak gives you a miserably itchy rash. Food's bad. Weak miners get sick and die. That's why there are almost never men older than thirty in the diggings."

"Why do you do it?" I asked.

"My brother and I have gold fever," he said with a grin.

I led the mules alongside the stream and watched as the Yankee boy poured shovel loads of dirt and rocks into canvas bags and dragged them down to the water.

"If my brother and I had a wooden rocker, we could wash a lot more gold. But rockers are expensive," said the boy, wiping the sweat from his forehead. He filled a shallow, wide-flared tin pan with dirt and creek water and gently twirled the pan, tipping the water out until only the heaviest bits remained. After sifting through the gravel with his fingers and pushing most of it over the side of the pan, some glinting particles remained.

"Gold," he said. "Worth about half a dollar."

"That's great!" I exclaimed. I was getting gold

fever myself. But a Spanish proverb floated into my mind. "A horse is worth more than riches." Fandango. She was more precious to me than gold.

"Have you ever heard of the bandit Joaquín Murieta?" I asked.

"Of course. He's famous."

"Do you know where his hideout is?" I asked.

"I heard it's somewhere near Angel's Camp. Why?" he asked.

"Just curious," I answered. I certainly didn't want Murieta to hear that a boy was asking about the location of his hideout. I tried to hide my excitement. Angel's Camp was a town not far from Sonora.

We talked for another hour while the boy dug and washed more dirt. He didn't find any more gold while I was watching.

I had to leave because there was no grass for the mules to graze on in Plug-Ugly. Just before nightfall I found a grassy area surrounded by trees. I unpacked, hobbled the mules, and made dinner. I fell asleep under the stars, listening to the calls of night birds and dreaming of Fandango.

During that fall, I asked about Murieta at all the camps. I heard stories about him but no more about the location of his hideout.

At the beginning of winter, I brought the mules back to Stockton. They traveled quickly because their packs were almost empty. They carried only my food, clothing, and Pedro's growing bag of gold. I worried about bandits. Luckily, I hadn't met any so far.

I entered the Stockton store that Pedro had told

me about. Looking at the mining equipment, blankets, and clothing, I wandered among the red and blue flannel shirts, wool pants, high boots, and broad-brimmed felt hats. I was amazed at the prices. Good boots were fifty dollars. A wool hat cost twelve dollars and a comb two dollars. A candle cost one dollar. A frying pan was six dollars, a coffee pot ten dollars.

The owner, a tall blond man, said, "Can I help you?"

I gave him Pedro's list of supplies with the prices I was to pay written next to each item.

"I remember No Go Pedro. Quite a character," he chuckled.

"He's hurt. I'm taking over for him until he's better," I explained.

The storekeeper collected my supplies and carried them to the front porch. He didn't seem concerned that I was so young. Many boys had come to the gold country where they enjoyed more freedom than they were used to. Some became orphans during the hard trek from the East. A few turned lawless.

Many canvas sacks held food that was dried or preserved: salt pork, bacon, canned meat and fish, dried beans, split peas, rice, dried apples, and raisins. Other sacks held items that kept for long periods of time, such as coffee, sugar, molasses, tobacco, cornmeal, and ingredients for sour dough bread. Four sacks held oats for the mules.

I bought a warm, red and blue wool serape that covered my whole body. It was as thick as a blanket with a slit for my head. I also bought two more packages of bullets.

The storekeeper added up the cost of each item. I checked the bill and paid it in gold dust.

"Are you going near Indian Gulch?" he asked.

I checked my tattered map. "Yes. But not for a month."

"That's fine. You're the only one I know who is going there. A Señor Sosa is looking for gold somewhere between Indian Gulch and Poverty Hill. A lawyer in San Francisco sent me this urgent letter for him. I will give you eight dollars to deliver it. If Pedro trusts you, I trust you. Here," he said, handing me a small sack of coins and the letter.

"I'll do my best," I said.

I loaded the supplies on the mules. My muscles had grown stronger during the fall. But I knew the mules weren't pleased with their heavy loads. Jobo raised a back hoof in warning. Gina's thin tail slapped back and forth in irritation. Elsa pinned her ears back menacingly. Fabio's clenched jaw and fixed stare told me exactly what he thought of his full pack. I was glad mules couldn't talk.

FIVE

SCURVY

O N MY RETURN JOURNEY TO THE GOLD camps, I passed herds of mule deer coming down from their summer ranges on the western slope of the Sierra Nevada. The white peaks of the Sierra sparkled in the distance.

Visiting more camps on Pedro's map, I marveled at the conditions the miners endured. They would stand in icy streams, bent over, for ten or twelve hours a day, panning for gold. They slept in shacks or tents. Often their food was rotten. They rarely had fruits or vegetables.

The miners were always joyous to see my packed mules. They were also starved for company and ready to talk. One Yankee told me that Murieta had been seen riding a beautiful palomino. Fandango!

Most of the Yankee miners weren't planning to stay in California long, so they had no desire to build towns or communities. The homes they longed for, and told stories about, were back east. When the gold ran out, the miners were quick to abandon their camps.

Some mining towns were already ghost towns by the end of 1852, when I passed through them. It was spooky to enter what had once been a town. Rusty, broken tools littered the creek beds. Empty cans and garbage marked where the camps had been. The abandoned shacks looked forlorn.

When I first came across Señor Sosa's camp, I thought it was deserted. I had crossed between Indian Gulch and Poverty Hill twice, looking for the man. I was ready to give up when a downpour started, and I saw a broken down shack. As I hobbled and unloaded the mules a short distance away, I heard a low moan. I pushed the door of the shack open. Inside was dark. A nauseating stench, like a decaying corpse, almost knocked me backwards.

"Hello? Who are you?" a weak voice asked in Spanish.

"My name is Mateo."

"You must be an angel. Good. I'm finally dying."

"No. I'm not an angel. I'm an arriero," I replied.

"My name is Sebástiano Sosa."

I had found my man.

"Are you sick or hurt?" I asked, knowing it must be one or the other.

"Sick."

Even though it was pouring rain, I hesitated to enter the shack.

"Do you have cholera or dysentery or malaria? I have quinine. It can ease malaria."

"I don't have malaria."

I pushed down my fear of the deadly cholera and entered the shack. He had not been able to get up from his bed. His shack smelled of vomit, urine, and

diarrhea. I breathed through my mouth to avoid the overwhelming odors.

I had never seen anyone in such awful condition. His bleeding gums made his attempt to smile ghastly. His skin had a purple hue. His arms were swollen to double their normal size. They were black where his blood vessels had broken. He was hideous. But as I moved closer, I could see what was wrong with him.

"What have you been eating?" I asked.

"Nothing lately. Before that only spoiled salt pork and flour fried in grease," he said weakly.

"For how long?" I asked.

"Months," he said.

"Were you always alone?" I said.

"No. I had a partner. We had studied law together before the gold rush. We met again in the diggings. But he gave up this summer. We hadn't found any gold, and our food was running out. He left for San Francisco to start a law firm. I planned to follow him back in a few weeks to become his law partner."

"Why didn't you?" I asked.

"I found gold. Not much. But enough to keep me here panning. After a few months I got sick. My arms and legs swelled. Now it hurts me to move," he said.

"You have scurvy. I've seen it in other camps where the miners don't have good food. You're the worst case I've ever seen."

The watery brown eyes pleaded, "Can you help me?"

"Yes. You need fruits and vegetables. I have

some in my packs. I'll stay until you are strong enough to take care of yourself."

The sick man lay back and closed his eyes. "God bless you. You are an angel," he murmured.

I brought him raisins and dried apples from Fabio's pack. I filled his cup with water and fed him. His breath stunk like an animal that had been dead for a month. He could barely chew and swallow. Was I too late?

"I can't make a fire to cook potatoes and onions for you until the rain stops. I'm going to hike around and see if I can find some wild greens. An old Indian showed me which plants cure scurvy."

I looked around for the plants. But I found nothing.

The rain had stopped by the time I returned. I took dry wood from inside the shack and built a fire outside. I fried a pan full of onions and potatoes. The wonderful aroma floated into the shack.

I brought a plate of vegetables to his bed.

"Smells good," said the grateful man.

"Eat as much as you can. It will make you better."

I fed him. But he wasn't able to chew much.

I noticed a copy of *Robinson Crusoe* and three law books on a crude wooden shelf. The law books reminded me of the letter. *I'll wait until he's stronger*, I thought. *It might be bad news.*

I slept outside the door. I couldn't stand the smell in the shack.

The sick man seemed a little better in the morning and ate more of the onions and potatoes. I heated the dried fruit in water until it became plump and easier for him to swallow.

After breakfast I moved the mules to a new place to graze and informed them that they had the rest of the week off. I returned to the shack.

"Can you walk outside so I can clean your cabin? You can lean on me."

"I'll try," Señor Sosa replied weakly.

After I settled him in the sunshine, I cleaned his shack. Señor Sosa looked spent when I helped him back inside and settled him in his clean bed. He slept all afternoon.

The next morning I helped him peel off his dirty clothes, wash, and put on clean ones. After I fed him lunch I asked, "Would you like me to read you *Robinson Crusoe?*"

"That would ease my suffering, Mateo, my angel."

After I had read for about an hour, a movement in a shadowy corner of the cabin caught my eye. I saw a small, sleek animal slink out of a hole under the crude boards and bound gracefully onto Señor Sosa's bed.

"Is that supposed to be in here?" I asked, pointing to the small animal with round, bright eyes. It looked like a tiny raccoon, only cuter, and its coat was softer.

Señor Sosa smiled. "She's my pet," he said as he stroked her velvet fur. "Madalena was my only companion before you came. She's a ringtail. They're so good at catching rats and mice that they're often called miner's cats. This cabin would be overrun with rodents if she didn't eat them."

"She's pretty," I said.

"Madalena has been a great comfort. I figured she'd keep the rodents off my corpse. I'd been warned that one in five miners died in the first year of the gold rush. I didn't believe it. Now I wonder how so many survived."

I reached out a hand to pet the glossy fur. But Madalena darted off the bed and down the hole.

The next morning the lawyer was noticeably healthier. *He's a young man*, I realized with amazement. *It's time*, I decided.

"I have a letter for you," I announced after he fed himself breakfast.

Señor Sosa stared at me in surprise.

"It's from your partner in San Francisco. He said it's important. I kept it until you were strong, in case it's bad news."

"Read it to me, Mateo. I am still weak."

"Yes, señor. The letter is dated September 15, 1852."

"What month is it now, Mateo?"

"December, señor."

"Continue."

I read: " *'My Friend, I hope this letter finds you in good health.'* "

The lawyer snorted. "Go on," he urged.

Please join me in San Francisco immediately. Because we are Spanish-speaking lawyers, who also speak English, we are needed to help rancheros to prove in court that they own the land they live on.

Disappointed Yankee miners often want land in California. They have pressured the American government to issue the Land Act of 1851. It requires all rancheros to submit proof, within two years, that their land was given to them by the Spanish or Mexican governments. Often the land grants are not well documented so lawyers and courts find it easy to detect some flaw in the titles. Many Californios have already lost part or all of their ranchos. Others don't realize that their ranchos are in danger.

The court's deadline is approaching. I have too much business to handle by myself. It cannot wait. I need your help. Please join me in San Francisco. I anxiously await you.

Sincerely,
Your Partner,
Manuel Torres Vargas

After I finished reading him the letter, we sat in stunned silence.

I spoke first. "The rancho I grew up on might be in danger."

In my daydreams, I was mayordomo of the rancho. Fandango was my horse. Now this dream might never come true.

"It is important for theranchero to hire a lawyer and show his documents of ownership in court before the deadline," said Señor Sosa. "Otherwise he could lose his rancho. Thousands of rancheros will be affected by this new law."

Señor Sosa ate well at breakfast the next morning. He was talkative, and he looked better.

"How did you become an arriero, Mateo?"

I explained about my father's death and Fandango's theft. "I'm going to take my horse back from Murieta as soon as I find out where his hideout is. Do you know?" I asked eagerly.

"No. Sorry. I wish there were some kindness I could do for you now. But there is a time for everything."

"My father used to tell me that," I said.

The lawyer smiled. His gums looked healthier. "Write down my partner's address in San Francisco. You can find me there if you need me. I'm leaving here as soon as I'm able. Will you sell me a mule? I have gold. I'll pay you twice what it is worth. That should satisfy its owner. Please?"

"Yes, señor. And I'll sell you the food you will need. Tomorrow I must be on my way. There are miners waiting for supplies."

"Bless you, Mateo. Here, take this."

The lawyer gave me his copy of *Robinson Crusoe*.

"Thanks!" Books were hard to get in the diggings.

I sold Señor Sosa a large black mule named Yago. I left the next day. It was a long time before I would see the lawyer again.

SIX

LIGHTNING STORM

IF I HAD KNOWN HOW TERRIBLE THE WINter would be, I would never have volunteered to be Pedro's arriero. I didn't know enough to lead mules through the mountains this time of year. The first lightning storm proved that.

The mules and I were high in the foothills of the Sierra on a rainy January afternoon. Towering clouds hung above us. Below us stretched endless miles of forests and valleys cut by meandering streams. The mules carefully picked their way across a barren ridge. Large, heavy, widely spaced raindrops made the granite slick.

I felt a strange tingling on the back of my neck. I turned back in my saddle to watch the mules go over a mound of rocks on the trail. Jobo was teetering on his small hooves at the top of the pile. Suddenly from out of the heavens, a jagged bolt of lightning flashed down. For an instant I was blinded by the brightness. A loud CRACK exploded in my ears. Booming echoes followed. When I could see again, the lightning bolt was burned into my vision.

Jobo had collapsed. Terrified braying filled the air. I slid off Cisco and cautiously made my way

back down the line. I stroked and spoke to each mule as I passed on the narrow trail. Any of them could have crowded me off the trail and over the steep cliff. But none did.

I finally reached the fallen Jobo. I stared at his nostrils. No breath flared the edges. I lay my ear on his warm, wet belly. I heard nothing and felt no rise and fall. I smelled burning hair. "Jobo?" I cried. No response. I pulled the bowie knife out of my boot and cut the worn rope that attached Jobo to the other mules.

Elsa, the mule behind Jobo, leaned away from the body. The trail was too narrow for her to turn around and flee.

"It's all right, Elsa," I said gently. But it wasn't all right. And it was my fault. How could I have been so stupid? Jobo was on the highest point in the area. Of course the lightning bolt killed him. And if I didn't move the other mules down quickly, another bolt might strike any minute.

The mules in front of Jobo had already moved down the trail. But the ridge was too narrow, with sheer drops on both sides, for the mules behind Jobo to get around his corpse. And they didn't have enough room to turn around.

"Help me, Papá," I prayed. I folded Jobo's legs under him. There was no time to try to save his pack. With strength I didn't know I had, I rolled the heavy body off the trail. It started a rockslide as it fell. I looked away from the sickening sight to Elsa and the line of mules behind her. They were all staring over the cliff at their teammate's tumbling body.

"Come on, mules," I shouted through the rain. I led Elsa. The other mules followed. Another bolt of lightning leapt through the air, connecting sky and earth. Five seconds later the rolling boom of thunder echoed around the hills. I felt awful about Jobo's death.

I still felt sad a week later when I came across two starving miners. They staggered from their shack above a ravine, waving and shouting when they heard the mule's bell.

"Stop. Stop," they cried.

They were the thinnest men I had ever seen.

"We've run out of food."

"What would you like?" I asked.

A man with sunken cheeks and haunted eyes glanced nervously at his tall partner. "We don't have any money."

"I'll give you what you need," I said. It was Pedro's food, not mine to give away. But I was sure Pedro would do the same. "I'll give you enough to last you both for two weeks so you can get back to Jamestown."

"But, we ain't goin' back," said the man with the hollow cheeks.

"Frank," interrupted the taller man. He had a crazy look in his red-rimmed blue eyes. "That'll do."

"But you said . . ." Frank began to argue.

The tall man gave Frank a chilling stare. "Shut up." They took the food I offered, but I had an unpleasant feeling about these two Yankees. I repacked the mules and left, wanting to put as much distance between the men and me as I could. But darkness comes early in the winter. Soon I had to make camp for the night.

I fed the mules oats from their packs for dinner because there was no grass. I had a hard time getting to sleep. Every moving bough, animal call, or snapping twig in the thick pine forest made me nervous.

I awoke to the touch of a cold Colt revolver against my cheek. It was Frank, the miner. His hand shook. I didn't move. But he knew I was awake.

"We ain't leaving until we find gold," he rasped. Frank was crazy or desperate or both. So was his partner.

"We'll take this mule," the tall man said. "Put the pack with the beef jerky on him. If you try anything or follow us, we'll kill you."

I believed him. I put the pack with the dried beef on Fabio. It wasn't his pack. There was no tobacco in it.

Fabio was reluctant to leave the other mules. Frank pulled and his partner pushed and they both swore.

"All mules this stubborn?" Frank asked his partner.

"Don't know. Ain't been around mules much," the tall man replied.

When they were gone, my racing heart calmed. I wouldn't try to rescue Fabio. I felt lucky to be alive. I remembered my father's words: "Desperate men do desperate things."

Two days later, I looked back at the line of mules as it snaked around some rocky hills dotted with a few scraggly pines. There was Fabio, lead rope dragging, in his usual place at the end of the line. I stopped Cisco and dismounted. I pulled a wad of tobacco out of Paz's pack and made my way down the line to Fabio. "Chewing tobacco is a disgusting habit," I scolded him fondly.

Fabio took the tobacco from my palm and gave me a knowing look. I wished he could talk.

Fabio saved my life early that spring.

When the snow in the Sierra melted, every tiny creek became a river. Roaring, rushing rivers flooded gorges and gulches. The powerful currents tore trees out by their roots and destroyed several camps. Sometimes I would ride to where there had once been a camp and see nothing but water churning through a canyon.

One bright blue March day, I was gazing at the dazzling whiteness of the mountain peaks in the distance. Blue lupine and orange California poppies splashed the green foothills around me with color. Sunshine warmed my back as I rode Cisco. It was a relief after the cold, damp winter.

The trail led us far down into a shadowed canyon. Cisco flicked his ears nervously as we walked across the bare granite bottom. I turned in my saddle to look at the other mules. Their ears were pointed up the canyon. Some had stopped.

I heard a rumble. Thunder? I didn't know what

the noise was. But it was getting louder.

I kicked Cisco hard with both heels. He was starting up the trail worn in the opposite wall when a torrent of water tore through the canyon. The raging water smacked me off Cisco and pulled me under, tumbling me against the granite sides and bottom of the canyon. I fought to the surface. I caught a glimpse of the mules struggling under their packs. The worn rope that had strung them together had broken. Luckily, they were not fully loaded, and they could swim. I could not. As the current pushed me through the canyon, it dragged me under again and threw me against a mule.

Frantically, I tried to grab onto it. My hand closed on something thin. A rope? No, a tail. I held on, trying to keep my head above water. The mule fought the current with more strength than I had. The churning torrent shoved us along as it roared out of the canyon into a wider area. There, with more room to spread out, it lost force and the mule was able to drag me up onto what was now a wide bank above the water. I saw that the mule was Fabio. I let go of his tail and threw up a belly full of river water. The floodwater rushed by as I counted the mules from my hands and knees. One was missing.

I looked down river. Trees littered the new riverbanks. One of the trees moved as the current, slower now, swirled around it. I wiped the wet hair out of my eyes and looked again. It was not a tree—it was a mule. I shakily got to my feet and made my way along the bank. Only the mule's belly showed above the muddy water. I splashed into the water, reached around the mule's neck, and heaved her head out. I gasped. "Oh Elsa." No pulse beat under my hands as I fought the current for her body. I was only strong enough to drag her head and neck up on the shore. Water flowed around her body, trying to tug her from my grasp.

I cradled Elsa's head in my lap. Tears ran down my cheeks as I stroked her neck. "Elsa, you were a good mule," I whispered into her limp ear. "I'm so sorry."

SEVEN

CREEK OF THE DEAD

IT WAS JULY OF 1853, WHEN I FINALLY returned to Sonora. Gina's bell announced our arrival.

No Go Pedro limped into the street to meet us. "Mateo! My mules!" he shouted.

"You sound surprised," I said accusingly.

"No, no." He paused. "Nine mules?"

"I'm sorry. It was my fault. Lightning killed Jobo, and Elsa was killed in a flash flood."

"Accidents happen, Mateo," said Pedro kindly.

"Yago is still alive. I sold him to a miner who had scurvy and needed to return to San Francisco. The man paid double what the mule was worth. He seemed like a good man, and he needed Yago."

"That's all right then," said Pedro. "You can hobble the mules outside of town. Emilio's son will watch them, so you can come to the house and tell me your adventures."

The aroma of spicy frijoles simmering met me at the door. Pedro sat in a high-backed chair. He didn't look good. I told him about the lightning storm, the flash flood, the lawyer with scurvy, the two crazy miners, and how Fabio came back.

"Those challenges made a man out of you, Mateo," said Pedro proudly.

At dinner, Emilio's wife served me frijoles, stewed beef, tortillas, and rice. Sitting down to a home cooked meal made me miss the rancho. Now, more than ever, I was determined to find Fandango.

"Have you heard any news of Murieta?" I asked at the table.

"Yes," answered Pedro. The old man looked troubled.

"Well?" I said impatiently.

"A man in town saw Murieta in Angel's Camp less than a month ago. He raved about the beautiful palomino horse Murieta rode. He said Murieta's hideout is in a place called Los Muertos Creek, Creek of the Dead. There are many people there. They are all Mexicanos or Californios who are loyal to Murieta. That is where Murieta keeps the stolen horses," said Pedro.

"Murieta's hideout!" I leapt up, knocking my chair over in excitement. "I'll leave tomorrow. Can you show me where Los Muertos Creek is on the map?"

Pedro, Emilio, his wife, and son looked at me as if I were going to my own funeral.

"You will be shot, Mateo. Murieta has many guards. You cannot hope to get near your horse. And even if you did succeed in getting back your mare, Murieta would hunt you down and kill you," said Emilio.

"Go back to your rancho. You have done a good

job for me. With your half of the profits you could buy a fine horse and return to the rancho with plenty of gold. Please, Mateo. Let Murieta keep the palomino," begged Pedro.

"No," I replied. "Fandango is the only family I have left. She means more to me than anything in the world."

"More than life itself?" asked Pedro gently.

"Yes."

"Then this is good bye. Go with God. Thank you for being my arriero. You did well. Even better than I expected. I have not done as well. My leg is not good. My brother has invited me to stay here. It is time for the mules and me to retire. Thanks to you I have enough money to buy some land outside of town for my favorite mules. I will sell the others."

"Will you keep Fabio?" I asked anxiously.

"Yes. I'll keep Fabio. And a large supply of chewing tobacco," he chuckled. "You didn't like Fabio when you left here. I'll bet he taught you a lesson or two."

I nodded.

"Patience and loyalty, perhaps? You seem stronger and wiser after your time as an arriero. I would willingly trust the Mateo I see before me with my mules. I was not so sure the young pup you were a year ago could handle the job. But you grew into it. You have proven to be honest and courageous." The old arriero sighed. "If only you had gained the wisdom to avoid a fight when you are overmatched."

The next morning I purchased enough food for

two weeks, two canteens, saddlebags, and a pistol. I bought a bridle trimmed with silver for Fandango.

I brushed and patted each mule for the last time, whispering a parting insult into each pair of long ears. I lingered over Fabio, stroking his neck sadly. He looked at me with a steady, ox-like gaze. Finally he pushed me with his nose, as if to say, "Go."

I filled the canteens with water and stuffed my clothes, *Robinson Crusoe*, food, the bridle, and my new pistol into the saddlebags. I felt like a poorly packed mule with the bags slung over my shoulder.

Three days later, I passed near Angel's Camp. I didn't want to attract any attention, so I stayed out of the town.

Late the next morning, I came to Los Muertos Creek. I heard voices and horses moving through the brush. "There he is!" someone yelled.

Had they seen me?

Shouts rang out. They were challenged by the low, blood-curdling growl of a grizzly bear.

I hid in the brush, but I had a clear view of the bear. No one would notice me. All eyes were on the huge grizzly. The bear showed his long teeth and pink gums as the horses and riders surrounded him. He let out a menacing rumble.

The huge grizzly stood up on his back legs. He was at least ten feet tall. And there was Fandango being ridden by Murieta! The grizzly loomed over them. I couldn't breathe. Had I come all this way to watch my horse die? Even the bandits were silent and still, as they watched the bear. The grizzly

swayed slightly back and forth over the horse and rider. He peered at them through small black eyes. Suddenly Three-Fingered Jack's braided leather reata hissed through the air from behind him. The second the bear was distracted, Murieta threw his reata. Both loops fell around the bear's neck. As Murieta and Three-Fingered Jack held the bear between them with their taut reatas, a cheer went up from the bandits. The bear lowered and tried to lunge, first at Three-Fingered Jack's pinto horse, next at Fandango. But the reatas, which were wrapped around their saddle horns, held.

Murieta smiled and began joking about the bull and bear fight they would watch that night. I wanted to strangle him. The handsome bandit wore a coat of bull hide. But Fandango had no protection from the teeth and claws of the bear. Her eyes and nostrils were wide with fear. She was tied to a grizzly bear!

The bear sat back on his haunches. Three-Fingered Jack's rope went slack for a moment. Suddenly, in a rolling motion of muscle, the grizzly came at Fandango. He sliced her with his long, curved claws. Fandango jumped backward. Three-Fingered Jack tightened his rope and held the grizzly away from her. Murieta was no longer smiling. His dark eyes blazed with fury. He reached his hand down to touch Fandango's shoulder. His hand came back red with her blood.

"*¡Vámanos!*" shouted Murieta angrily. "Pablo, you ride ahead of the bear on the way back to the hideout. Luis, throw another reata around the grizzly's neck and follow."

I watched as Pablo rode his gray horse close in front of the bear to lure him on. The bandits slackened their reatas. The bear shook his head and sprang forward at Pablo's mount. The mare quickly leaped ahead, away from the bear. Her rider brought her close to the bear again. The bear lunged forward after the gray horse. In this slow manner, the grizzly followed the bandits to Murieta's hideout. The bandits chained the bear in a pit.

I knew what the bandits had planned for the bear. They would tie the hind leg of the grizzly to the front leg of a wild bull and bet on which would kill the other. I hated these bloody fights.

Near sunset, I heard the fight. The cheers of the bandits didn't hide the growling and bellowing of the enraged, wounded animals. At last the shouts of the bandits died away. I heard only the roar of the grizzly. He had won. Three gunshots echoed off the hills. Silence.

EIGHT

I HID IN THE TREES AND BRUSH UNTIL nightfall, listening to guitar music, laughter, and drunken singing. A full moon rose. I followed Los Muertos Creek uphill and away from Murieta's camp. I discovered Fandango and the other horses grazing in a wide, grassy meadow surrounded by dense pine trees. None of the horses were hobbled. Except for the new slash, Fandango looked in good shape, muscular and glossy. Murieta must have prized her and treated her well.

A guard walked unsteadily around the herd. Fandango raised her head and looked at him. He looked back through bleary eyes, drawled, "Beautiful horse," and sang her a Mexican love song in a quivering voice. He was drunk.

The guard sat down with his back against a tree not far from me. A rifle lay across his lap. As I crouched on the damp ground, I heard my father's calm voice. "Patience, Mateo. There is a time for everything."

I waited. My legs fell asleep. But I was still awake when the guard dozed off and began to snore.

Now was my time! But I was afraid to go out to

the horses in the moonlight. I might be seen. If only I could make the same whistle my father had used to call the mare. "Help me, Papá," I prayed. I whistled softly.

Fandango threw her head up. The rest of the horses grazed peacefully. Fandango's ears pricked toward me. She snorted, nostrils wide. Hesitantly, she walked to where I hid behind a bush. My heart was pounding so loudly I was afraid it would wake the guard.

I put my palm out flat so Fandango could smell me. She stood still as I eased the bit into her mouth and pulled the bridle up over her ears. I slid the saddlebags onto her broad back, grabbed the reins and a chunk of her thick, silver mane and swung my right leg over her back.

As soon as we were away from the herd I leaned forward and whispered, "Go." She shot off. She powered up the hills and flew over the valleys. We came to a level plain. I had been riding a mule for so long that I had almost forgotten the crazy joy and freedom of a flat-out gallop. But my soaring happiness was mingled with fear. At any moment a bandit might shoot me off Fandango's back.

I didn't slow Fandango until I felt her tire. I searched until I found the perfect place to hide. Tree branches, bushes, and vines covered the space between two steep hills. I guided Fandango into the mass of green leaves. Even though I leaned down on her shoulder, I was almost swept off. The mare became tangled, but, just as she was starting to panic,

she broke through. Stretched before us was a small valley with a tinkling stream running through it.

I slid off Fandango and looked at her chest. The cuts from the grizzly's claws were bleeding again. I took off her bridle, and she rubbed her sweaty head against my shoulder. I scratched behind her ears and rubbed the sides of her mouth where the bit had pressed. When I finished, she turned to graze. Before I fell asleep I whispered, "I got her back, Papá. I got her back."

We stayed in the hidden valley until the mare's cuts healed. But we were both restless. When we started our journey, Fandango was eager to travel and seemed to enjoy the long trip back to the rancho. I did not. My fear turned every motion or sound into a bandit waiting to shoot me. The trip took us more than two weeks because I became lost several times.

I didn't relax until I saw the rancho's long, low adobe house with its red tile roof and wide veranda in the distance. At last I was coming home with my father's horse. I was safe—as safe as I would ever be while Murieta lived.

Suddenly two bullets whizzed by me. Fandango jumped in surprise. A voice from behind a far pile of rocks shouted, "Halt."

A vaquero stepped from behind the rocks with his rifle pointed at me. His chestnut horse stood quietly behind him. This was not the homecoming I had expected.

"Miguel! It's me, Mateo," I called.

"Mateo? Yes, it is you," he said, lowering his

rifle. "Your shoulders are broader and you are taller. But I should have recognized Fandango." He mounted his horse and rode to me. He looked older and smaller than I remembered.

"Please pardon me. I am an old man and my eyesight is not good."

"So I see. You weren't trying to hit me, were you?"

"No. I'm a better shot than that," he laughed. "It is good to see you, Mateo. Why did you leave the rancho so suddenly? We were all so worried about you."

"I'm sorry you were worried, but I had to. It's a long story. I'll explain it all to you and Don Rafael."

We walked our horses side by side toward the whitewashed rancho house.

"You have grown," said Miguel with a twinkle in his eyes. "The señoritas will find you handsome."

I felt blood rush to my face and changed the subject.

"Can I work here as a vaquero, Miguel?"

"Yes, of course. I am delighted."

Don Rafael welcomed me joyfully. I told Miguel and Don Rafael about the mysterious vaquero who had threatened to steal Fandango, Murieta's theft of Fandango, and my year as an arriero.

"Now I understand why you left so suddenly and why José never returned," said the ranchero.

So it had been José! I never liked him. He had a way of staring at me that made me feel uncomfortable. He had been jealous of my father's position as mayordomo of the rancho, and Papá had warned me to stay away from him.

"José will never return. Murieta killed him," I explained. "Don Rafael, I bring danger with me. If Murieta discovers that Fandango is here, he may try to steal her," I warned.

"Mateo, this is your home. Your father was my trusted friend. We will defend you and Fandango for as long as I own the rancho," he assured me. "Unfortunately, that may not be long." Worry made him frown.

"Won't you always own the rancho?" I asked in surprise.

"Maybe not. Yankees are trying to steal my land. My neighbor to the north has lost his. A few Yankees have already settled on the eastern edge of my land and begun to farm it. These squatters are sure the American courts will give them the title."

"Is that why you shot at me, Miguel? Did you think I was a Yankee?"

"Scaring them away is our only defense," said Don Rafael.

"No, it's not," I said. "I delivered a letter to a Californio lawyer in the gold diggings. His law partner begged him to come to San Francisco to help defend the Californios' land grants in court. Do you have proof of your land grants?"

"Yes, papers. But I do not trust the American courts. They will find a way to take my land."

"The lawyer I met would help us. When I found him, he was dying of scurvy. He was grateful for my food and care. Take him the papers soon, before it is too late," I said.

"I don't think it will do much good. If the Yankees want my land, they will take it."

"Don Rafael, most of the Yankees I have met are law abiding. If the court supports your ownership, the Yankees will leave you alone."

"I hope you are right, Mateo. I fear you are not. Anyway, I am too old for the long ride to bring the papers to the lawyer in San Francisco. And why should he help me? You are the one he would help."

I knew he was waiting for me to volunteer. I didn't. After an uncomfortable silence, Don Rafael left the room and returned holding age-yellowed papers. "Mateo, will you take my papers to San Francisco?" he asked.

It was the question I dreaded. "I don't want to ride Fandango to San Francisco. Murieta may find us. We are safer on the rancho," I confessed shamefacedly.

"Please, Mateo. There are surely many other rancheros trying to save their ranchos. You know this lawyer. I do not. You can rest Fandango for a week before you set out."

I noticed that I was stroking the soft fuzz above my upper lip, just as my father had stroked his mustache when he was deciding something important.

"Your father would have gone," said Don Rafael quietly.

He was right. "I'll go. The lawyer will help us, if I can get there without Murieta catching me," I said.

"Go with God. Take the papers. Guard them with your life. If they are lost, so is my rancho." Don

Rafael paused and smiled. "But enough serious talk for now. Won't you join my family for dinner?"

"Yes. Thank you."

I washed, and Miguel gave me bear grease to slick back my hair. But I was self-conscious about my travel worn clothes when I joined the ranchero and his family that night.

The cook made a delicious dinner. The plump woman teased as she served me: "You've grown, Mateo. I think you'd better buy some new clothes."

"He can buy clothes when he is in San Francisco," Don Rafael said. "He is leaving next week on important business for me."

His wife nodded politely. Doña Dolores' perfume mixed with the aroma of the spicy food. She and her three young daughters wore fine silk dresses with ruffles at the cuffs and necks. The oldest daughter glanced at me shyly with large brown eyes under thick black lashes. The girl's hair, the rich color of a black mink, was so long that she had pushed it to the side so she would not sit on it.

Women were uncommon in the diggings, so I was not used to their company. I liked it.

We ate a beef stew with cabbage, rice with onions, soup, and tortillas. When dinner was over, I thanked Doña Dolores for the meal.

"You are welcome, Mateo. I hope it does you much good," she answered. Her silver necklace and earrings glittered in the candlelight.

"Will you please excuse me? I want to check on Fandango," I said. I gave a brief smile and a nod to the oldest señorita as I rose from the table. She quickly looked down at her untouched white frosted cake. But I saw her mouth curve in a smile.

"There's one more thing, Mateo," said Don Rafael. "Miguel tells me he is getting too old to be the mayordomo. So when you come back from San Francisco, he will begin to train you for the job. I am sure that in a few years you will make a fine mayordomo. Your father would be proud of you, Mateo."

"Thank you," I said quietly, afraid my voice would show my emotion.

For the next week, I slept in Fandango's stall. Whenever I heard rustling in the barn I clutched the pistol under my blanket.

Seven days after I had arrived back at the rancho, I woke before dawn to pack food in my saddlebags and feed Fandango. When the morning dew was still on the grass, I mounted the mare and left the rancho. It took me five days of hard riding to reach San Francisco.

NINE

THE HEAD IN THE JAR

COLD, SWIRLING FOG COVERED SAN Francisco. I could barely make out the masts of the tall sailing ships in the bay. The city was even larger than I had pictured. Brick buildings, several stories high, lined the wide streets. Red, white, and blue flags flew from many of them. Men from many countries hurried around. I saw no women.

The young city rang with the noise of carriages and construction. On the hills, men blasted out rock to make room for more buildings. The clanging from foundries, where machines were manufactured for the mines, echoed through the foggy streets.

After much searching I located the lawyer's brick building on Sacramento Street. I circled the block and found a livery stable for Fandango. I hated to leave her, but I figured she was safer off the street in a stable. The stable boy who took her inside earned my respect with his lavish praise of her. "She's a beauty, she is. Haven't seen a finer horse in the city. I've got a big stall in the back that'll suit her. It'll be a pleasure to look after this one."

I left her in the stable and hurried to the lawyer's office. I didn't want to be away any longer than I had to. Opening the door of the red brick office building, I immediately knew I was in the right place. Madalena, the ringtail, darted past me and up Señor Sosa's arm. She peered out at me from behind the lawyer's ear.

"Get down, Madalena," the lawyer scolded. Madalena jumped gracefully to the floor.

The lawyer's face lit up when he saw me. "Mateo! My angel!"

Señor Sosa, dressed in a pressed white cotton shirt and the gray wool trousers of a Yankee suit, rose from his desk and embraced me warmly. I hardly recognized him. His dark, clear eyes sparkled with good health in his clean-shaven face.

"You look healthy," I said.

"I am well, thanks to you. Why are you here? Can I repay your kindness at last?"

"Yes, Señor. I have a great favor to ask. Don Rafael, who owns the rancho where I grew up, fears he will lose his land. He asks that you present his papers to the court. He will pay you generously." I handed him the papers.

Señor Sosa sat down and read through the papers. I sat in a chair by a window, stroked my upper lip, and worried about Fandango.

The lawyer looked at me with concern. "Mateo, you seem nervous. Are you in trouble with the law?" he asked gently.

His question surprised me. Could everyone see my worry? "No, señor. It is not the law I am afraid of. It is the bandit Murieta. Do you remember when

I told you about Murieta and his gang stealing my father's horse, Fandango?"

"I do. Go on."

"I stole her back."

Señor Sosa's eyebrows shot up in amazement.

"Fandango is in the O'Hara Livery Stable around the corner. Do you think she will be safe there while we talk? I'm afraid Murieta may find out that she is in San Francisco. Murieta might even be here now."

"Oh, I'm quite sure he's here. I've seen him myself. He and Three-Fingered Jack."

I jumped out of the chair, my heart pounding with terror.

"No, no, sit still," the lawyer said, a smile creeping across his face. "Murieta's head and Three-Fingered Jack's hand are floating in jars of gin on display a few blocks from here. A group of Rangers hunted them down and killed them."

My surprise and relief must have shown on my face.

Señor Sosa smiled again. "Mateo, now that you have nothing to fear from Murieta, would you consider staying here as my apprentice? You're capable, heaven knows. You led a mule train through dangerous country. You're honest and reliable. You stayed with me and nursed me back to health. And you can speak and read both Spanish and English. You could become a fine lawyer here. Come with me when I present Don Rafael's papers in court tomorrow. Don't worry. The court will uphold his land rights."

What could I say? The lawyer was so generous.

Finally I spoke. "Thank you for your praise. But Don Rafael has offered me the position of mayordomo that my father held. When I finish in San Francisco, I'll return to the rancho to start my training. That is the life that I love."

Señor Sosa nodded wryly. "I would try to persuade you, but I see that your mind is made up. Don Rafael is lucky to have you. But for today and tomorrow, you'll be my guest. I'll show you San Francisco and treat you to dinner. But first I'll take you to see your old friend," said Señor Sosa, his eyes twinkling.

"Who? I don't know anyone in San Francisco," I said.

Señor Sosa grinned. "You'll see."

We left his office and walked away from the bay toward the brown hills. I barely noticed the buildings made of iron, adobe, canvas, wood, brick, and assorted ship parts. Was Señor Sosa taking me to see Three-Fingered Jack's hand and Murieta's head? I didn't want to look at the gruesome sight. I remembered how the young, handsome Murieta had said to me, "You remind me of myself at your age." I shivered in the August fog.

Señor Sosa panted as we walked up a steep hill at the edge of the city. "There he is." The lawyer pointed to a large pasture between the houses. Yago, the black mule I had sold Señor Sosa in the gold country, stood knee deep in oat grass.

Yago ambled over to meet me by the fence. I stroked his neck and looked him over. I leaned forward and whispered fondly into his long black ear,

"Your butt is even bigger than the last time I saw it."

Señor Sosa looked at me strangely, but I didn't care. I was lost in remembering No Go Pedro, my job as an arriero, and the year I grew to be a man.

AUTHOR'S NOTE

Thunder on the Sierra's main character, Mateo, was inspired by the life of Ignacio Villegas, who wrote about his experiences growing up on a rancho during the California gold rush. However, Mateo, his father, the arriero, the vaqueros, the miners, the ranchero and his family, and the lawyer are all fictional characters used to show what life was like for a Californio boy in the early 1850s.

The historical events that shaped Mateo's world did happen. In April 1850, the Foreign Miner's Tax, which charged foreigners twenty dollars a month for the right to mine gold, was passed. The Land Act of 1851 gave Californios, Spanish-speaking Californians, only two years to prove documentation of their land grants in Yankee courts.

Much as the first Spanish settlers had disregarded the land rights, culture, and customs of the Native Americans who originally inhabited California, so too the Yankees later often ignored the rights of the Spanish-speaking rancho owners of California. Many rancheros lost their land to Yankees during and after the gold rush.

Some of the characters in the book have some basis in actual history. According to California folklore, Joaquín Murieta, originally a Mexican miner, turned to a life of crime after being unjustly attacked by Yankee miners. The legendary Murieta, his gang of followers, and the bloodthirsty bandit Three-Fingered Jack murdered and stole from miners throughout the gold country.

In May of 1853 the California State Legislature

authorized Captain Harry S. Love and a group Rangers to capture the bandit Joaquín, dead or alive. What was said to be Murieta's head and Three-Fingered Jack's hand were exhibited in San Francisco in jars of alcohol until they were destroyed in the great earthquake of 1906.

CHRONOLOGY

May 1846	The U.S. declares war against Mexico.
January 1848	James Marshall finds gold at John Sutter's Mill.
February 1848	The Treaty of Guadalupe Hidalgo ends the war between the U.S. and Mexico.
March 1848	The *Californian*, a California newspaper, is the first to print the story of the gold discovery.
April 1850	The Foreign Miner's Tax is passed, charging "foreigners" twenty dollars a month for the right to mine gold.
September 1850	California is admitted as the thirty-first state of the United States.
March 1851	The Foreign Miner's Tax is repealed by state legislature.
Land Act of 1851	Rancheros have two years to prove they own their land.
July 1853	Harry Love and twenty other mountain rangers find what they claim to be Murieta's hideout and kill him and Three-Fingered Jack.
August 1853	The head and hand purported to belong to Murieta and Three-Fingered Jack are displayed in San Francisco floating in alcohol-filled glass jars.

- Bauer, Helen. *California Rancho Days*. Garden City, NY: Doubleday & Co., 1953.

- Harte, Bret. *Bret Harte's Gold Rush: "The Outcasts of Poker Flat," "The Luck of Roaring Camp," "Tennessee's Partner," and Other Favorites.* Berkeley: Heyday Books, 1997.

- Holliday, J.S. *The World Rushed In*. New York: Simon & Schuster, 1981.

- Jackson, Helen Hunt. *Ramona*. New York: Grosset & Dunlap, 1912.

- Ketchum, Liza. *The Gold Rush*. Boston: Little Brown, 1996.

- Kowalewski, Michael. *Gold Rush: A Literary Exploration*. Berkeley: Heyday Books, 1997.

- Lyngheim, Linda. *Gold Rush Adventure*. Van Nuys, CA: Langtry Publications, 1988.

- Marinacci, Barbara and Rudy. *California's Spanish Place-Names*. San Rafael, CA: Presidio Press, 1980.

- McNeer, May. *The California Gold Rush*. New York: Random House, 1950.

- Riley, Harvey. *The Mule*. New York: Dick & Fitzgerald Publishers, 1867.

SELECTED BIBLIOGRAPHY

• Sanderlin, George. *The Settlement of California.* New York: Coward, McCann & Geoghegan, 1972.

• Seidman, Laurence I. *The Fools of '49: The California Gold Rush, 1848-1856.* New York: Knopf, 1976.

• Sherrow, Victoria. *Life During the Gold Rush.* San Diego: Lucent Books, 1998.

• Shirley, Dame. *The Shirley Letters from the California Mines, 1851-1852.* New York: AA Knopf, 1949.

• Villegas, Ignacio. *Boyhood Days Reminiscences of California in the 1850's.* San Francisco: California Historical Society, 1983.

• Wellman, Paul I. *Gold in California.* Boston: Houghton Mifflin Company, 1958.